What if
your hair was
big
and **orange** and
really **bright?**

What if one eye was green and the other eye was blue as night?

What if you were quiet and very small? What if you were super, super, super, duper tall?

What if your **color** was unusual and **unique** in its own way?

What if

instead of standing still you liked to sway?

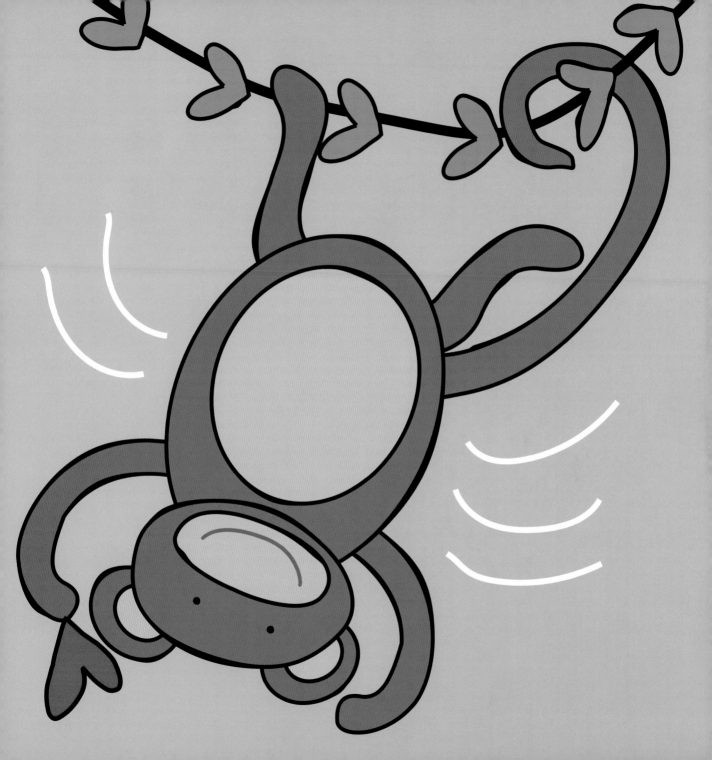

You see, being **different** is **special** and can give your spirit a **lift!**

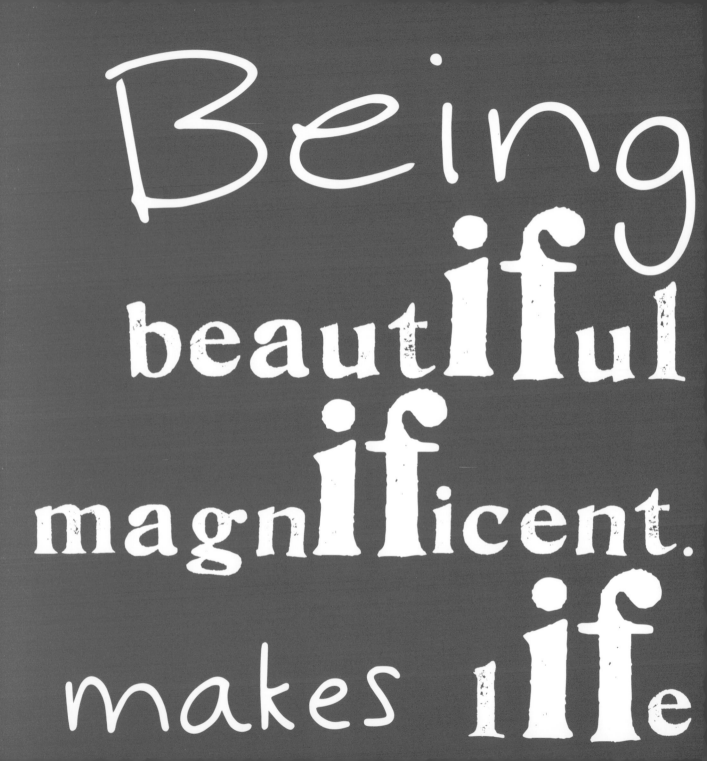

Being beautiful magnificent. makes life

different is and It's what a gift!

If all of us were exactly alike and totally the **same,** we'd be **boring** and **dull** and that would be a **shame.**

Everyone is Someone **special.** We are all **one of a kind.** Just show the world who you are—let your **you-ness shine!**

What if your **big** **orange** hair was the **perfect** place to **rest** a while?

What if the way you like to **sway** encouraged your friends to have **fun,** dance, and **play?**

blue

red

pink

and seeing you made everyone shout their **differences** out **loud?**

So, **what if** we **celebrate** each other, and what makes us **different,** too? 'Cause today is the **perfect** day to be **exactly** and **totally...**

Sandra Magsamen is a world-renowned artist, author, and designer whose products and ideas have touched millions of lives. Her books and stories are a heartfelt reminder that it's the people and moments in our lives that make life so wonderful!

Big heartfelt thanks to Karen Botti, Hannah Magsamen Barry, and Karen Shapiro. Their creativity and generous spirits are unique and valued gifts to me and the work we create in the studio.

Published by Sourcebooks Jabberwocky, an imprint of Sourcebooks, Inc.
P.O. Box 4410, Naperville, Illinois 60567-4410
(630) 961-3900
Fax: (630) 961-2168
sourcebooks.com

Library of Congress Cataloging-in-Publication Data is on file with the publisher.

Source of Production: 1010 Printing International, Kowloon, Hong Kong, China
Date of Production: October 2018
Run Number: 5013288

Printed and bound in China.
OGP 10 9 8 7 6 5 4 3 2 1